WILEY & GRAMPA'S CREATURE FEATURES

HAIR BALL FROM OUTER SPACE

WRITTEN AND ILLUSTRATED BY

KIRK SCROGGS

COUGHED UP FROM THE
DEPTHS OF TERROR!

LITTLE, BROWN AND COMPANY

New York ∾ Boston

In memory of Ruth Owens and Ann Richards. Two of Texas's finest.

Special thanks to:
Suppasak Viboonlarp, Mark Mayes, Hiland Hall, Amy Pennington, DJ Dave, Jackie Greed, Alejandra, Inge Govaerts, Joe Kocian, Jim Jeong, TJ, Irwin, Deep and Tabby, Will Keightly, Ruben Blades, Laura and Gus, Kyle and Natalie, Laura and Beth at the Grove, Kaman, Chevalier's Books, and the mezz crew—woo woo!

Andrea, Jill, Alison, Elizabeth, Saho, Sangeeta, and the Little, Brown Crew—yeeha!

An extra slimy alien thanks to Ashley and Carolyn Grayson, Harold and Betty Aulds, Dav Pilkey, and Steve Deline.

And an explosive three-bean thanks to Diane and Corey Scroggs.

Copyright © 2007 by Kirk Scroggs

Little, Brown and Company

Hachette Book Group USA
237 Park Avenue, New York, NY 10017
Visit our Web site at www.lb-kids.com

First Edition: May 2007

ISBN-13:978-0-316-05948-0 (hc) / ISBN-10: 0-316-05948-X (hc)
ISBN-13: 978-0-316-05949-7 (pb) / ISBN-10: 0-316-05949-8 (pb)

10 9 8 7 6 5 4 3 2 1

WORZ

Printed in the United States of America

Series design by Saho Fujii

The illustrations for this book were done in Staedtler ink on Canson Marker paper, then digitized with Adobe Photoshop for color and shade.
The text was set in Humana Sans Light and the display type was handlettered.

CHAPTERS

CHAPTER 1

Comin' at Ya!

Ladies and Gentlemen…A dangerous meteor, roughly the size of a mutated honeydew melon, is headed toward our planet as we speak! Scientists have tried to stop it with laser beams, nuclear weapons, and harsh language, but they've had no effect. The President advises that you all crawl into your underground bunkers and make sure they're stocked with medical supplies, wide-screen TVs, and, of course, plenty of delicious pork cracklins….

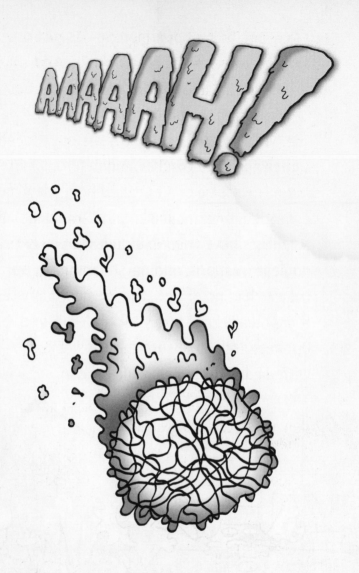

There's the meteor now! It's headed straight for us, bringing certain destruction and doom!

No, wait! That's not a meteor—it's just one of
Merle's world-famous hair balls. And that's
Dr. Nate Farkles, Gingham County's best
veterinarian, helping him cough it up. That's
me, Wiley, watching the disgusting procedure
with my grampa and gramma.

"Ooh! That reminds me," said Gramma, "we're
having Swedish meatballs with brown gravy
tonight. I've gotta stop by the grocery store."

But the streets of Gingham County were in chaos.

"Is it Mardi Gras again?" asked Grampa.

"No!" screamed a crazy screaming person.
"Haven't you heard? There's a meteor headed
this way. We have only a few minutes left!"

"Oooh!" said Gramma. "Then I'd better get to the grocery store, quick!"

"Stay calm!" yelled Officer Puckett. "Don't worry, folks. We have a team of top scientists and military leaders, and they have all assured me that there is nothing we can do and we're all gonna die!"

"I'm not gonna die!" yelled Grampa. "Not on Swedish meatball night!"

Grampa borrowed a grappling hook from the local sporting-goods store and flung it over a giant tennis racket on the roof.

"Pull it tight, Wiley," said Grampa. "We're gonna send that meteor back where it came from!"

"Aye, aye, Captain!" I yelled back.

We pulled the rope as hard
as we could.

Then Gramma used Merle to gnaw through the
rope, just as the meteor was about to hit.

The racket snapped back and smacked the you-know-what out of that meteor, sending it hurtling over a busload of nuns only to bounce off the Devil's Rump and crash into the wilderness.

That night, Grampa and I were a big hit on the
nightly news. Blue Norther even did a special
report on us.

"So that's it, folks! That's how my amazingly
accurate meteor prediction allowed these two
guys to save the town. Now, let's go live to the
scene of the impact...."

"After close examination with probes and beepy things," said Dr. Fred Yepsir, "we have concluded that the meteor is actually made of hair. That's right, it's a giant hair ball. Scientists are trying to determine if the hair is human or alien. We will also be giving it a shampoo and blow-dry."

"Hair!" yelled Gramma. "That reminds me. Tomorrow is haircut day. I made appointments for all of us!"

"Ohhh!" I moaned. The only thing I hate more than getting a haircut is a good tooth drilling.

CHAPTER 2

A Cut Above

The next day we headed over to Big Hair by Leslie, Gingham County's finest beauty salon.

"Let the boredom begin," I said as we went inside.

We were greeted by Leslie, the owner. "Bless your hearts! Pull up a chair. There're hairs to be cut."

"I'm not leaving until I look like the guy in this picture," said Grampa.

"Sugar," said Leslie, "I'm a stylist, not a miracle worker."

"It's a good thing you guys showed up," Leslie said as she worked my scalp into a luxurious lather. "That fancy new beauty shop opened up across the street this morning and has stolen all of my business. If this keeps up, I'll have to go back to my second job spinnin' records and spittin' phat lyrics on my beat box."

"You don't have to worry about us," said Grampa. "We would never get our beautiful do's done anywhere else. Isn't that right, Granny.... Granny?"

But Gramma was already walking toward Star Curls, mesmerized by its swirling lights and neon sign. It seemed like a lot of old ladies were headed over there.

They were greeted at the door by a seven-foot-
tall, rather odd-looking woman. "Greetings,
ladies. I am Jacqueline Greed, the most famous
hair stylist in the universe—I mean, world.
Please step into my beauty chamber for hair
follicle modification."

We tried to go in, too, but were stopped by the towering beautician.

"Sorry, gentlemen," said Madam Greed. "Only grandmas are allowed in my beauty chamber."

"That's all right," said Grampa nervously. "We already had our hair follicles modified, anyway. We'll just wait out in the car."

CHAPTER 3

I Can't Believe It's Not Gramma

After her haircut, Gramma just wasn't the same. She just stared straight ahead, blankly, and her hair was gi-normous!

"I dunno," said Grampa. "That new hairdresser was about as friendly as a constipated Komodo dragon."

Gramma's behavior just got weirder....

First, she tried to iron the wrinkles out of Merle's tail.

Then she fried some eggs with a homemade laser beam.

In the afternoon she got on the roof and tried to call someone named Slorzog.

Then her quilting buddies came over and they turned the backyard into a flying-saucer parking lot.

21

CHAPTER 4

Food Fright

That night she served us a home-cooked meal. "I made you a delicious garbanzo bean and raisin casserole," said Gramma robotically. "Bon appétit."

"Good, I'm starved," said Grampa. "All that napping I did today really gave me an appetite."

"Hmmm," I said. "Garbanzo bean and raisin casserole. Maybe Gramma is back to her old self."

Suddenly the casserole attacked Grampa, shooting out slimy tendrils of gravy and garbanzo bits! The goopy blob crawled right out of its dish!

"I always said your Gramma's cooking would be the death of me," yelled Grampa, "but this is ridiculous!"

Grampa jumped up and struck an impressive
martial arts pose.

"All right, you dastardly dish!" yelled Grampa.
"Now I'm gonna have to show you my Stinging
Scorpion maneuver!"

Grampa let the casserole have it, but his hand
just sliced right through the slime. Grampa's
skills had no effect!

And the same went for me. My Pulverizing Powerhouse kick didn't even slow the beastie down.

Even Merle's razor-sharp claws were useless.

We had to make a run for it. The killer casserole chased us right up the stairs.

"What should we do?" I asked.

"What we always do after one of your Gramma's meals," said Grampa. "Head straight for the bathroom!"

We barricaded ourselves in the bathroom.

"I've got an idea!" I said, opening the medicine cabinet. "What's the one substance that can combat the effects of Gramma's cooking?"

"Pepty Bizmo!" said Grampa. "Wiley, you're a genius. Here's the plan: I'll let the casserole in, and you can douse it with the pink stuff while I run to safety."

The casserole burst in and I poured the whole bottle of Pepty Bizmo on its pulsating head. It jiggled and shrieked, and then exploded.

"That cursed entrée can never harm another child!" I yelled triumphantly.

"I apologize for the behavior of your dinner,"
said Gramma. "I don't know what happened.
It was a new recipe."

"Don't sweat it, dear," said Grampa.
"It's okay. But I think tomorrow night we're
ordering a pizza."

We decided to spend the night out in my deluxe tree house.

"I don't know," said Grampa. "It looks like Gramma, sounds like Gramma, and cooks disgusting cuisine like Gramma, but it just isn't Gramma."

CHAPTER 5

Gross Anatomy

The next morning, we took what was left of the casserole to the authorities, who brought in some top experts—Dr. Hans Lotion and his grandson, Jurgen.

"I thought you were a foot doctor," said Grampa.

"Vell," said Hans, "vhen I'm not treating foot fungus, I like to dissect slimy critters. It helps me to relax."

Hans pulled out a scalpel and started to make
his incision. "First, I vill slice through ze flaky
crust and dig deep into ze jelly-like innards."

"Bingo!" said Hans, pulling out a large, drippy
organ. "Look at zis beauty! Zis is no ordinary
casserole. Beneath ze onions and rich brown
gravy, zere is a functioning heart."

"And here is ze source of power for ze organism. Zis indicates zat it vas created by no ordinary grandma-ma—it vas created by somevone with a superhuman, perhaps alien, intelligence.

"And here ve have ze brain of ze casserole. Zis little slimy organ is ze center of—No, vait. My bad. It's just a potato."

"Vell, gentlemen," said Hans. "My vork here is done. Now, if you'll excuse us. Ve have a plane to catch."

"You're flying to Washington to tell the President about these important findings?" asked Grampa.

"Are you kidding?" said Hans. "Zere are killer casseroles on ze loose. Ve are getting ze heck out of here!"

CHAPTER 6

Widespread Panic

It turns out we weren't the only ones with gramma problems. The next day at school, the lunchroom was abuzz with stories of grammas gone wild.

"Last night I was attacked by my grandmother's homemade cherry pie, via remote control!" yelled Hiland Hall.

"This morning my granny knit me a sweater that was not only horribly ugly, but it tried to eat me!" said little Amy Pennington.

"My nana came after me with toxic fu-fu-smellin' hand lotion, but she usually does that anyway," said Jubal, my best friend in all of Gingham County.

"This is crazy!" I yelled. "Grammas are supposed to be cool. Some strange force is turning our beloved grannies into dangerous criminals."

"Silence," said a mysterious nerd that walked up all of a sudden. "We can't talk here. We're being watched."

Sure enough, we were being watched closely by
Ms. Thang, the second-grade teacher. I couldn't
help but notice her fancy, big new hairdo.

"Come!" said the nerd. "Let's go talk where
it's safe."

We relocated to the playground, which was free of elderly women.

"Welcome, comrades," said the nerd. "I am Morbius and we are known as the **D**ragons, **W**izards, **E**lves, **E**xtraterrestrials, and **B**igfoot **S**ociety, or **D.W.E.E.B.S.** for short.

"Ever since the arrival of that meteor, our precious grandmas have become diabolical fiends," he said.

"Where do you think the meteor came from?" I asked.

"Who's to say?" said Morbius. "Saturn? Neptune? Perhaps it flew straight out of Uranus! What I do know is that the strange new beauty shop opened up the day after the meteor hit, and it's been a hoppin' granny hangout ever since. I implore all of you, keep an eye on your grandmas. Watch their every move. Alien forces are at work!"

STAR CURLS

FLASH LIGHT FOR SCARY EFFECT

CHAPTER 7

Stakeout

That night, we gathered our spy equipment to monitor Gramma's strange activities.

"Okay," said Grampa. "We'll communicate with these walkie-talkies. If I say 'The hen has flown the coop,' that means 'Gramma has left the building.' If I say 'Code blue,' that means 'We've got trouble.' And if I say 'The rooster needs a yellow melted,' that means 'Please bring me a grilled cheese sandwich, pronto!'"

Jubal and I used the doghouse as our base of operations. We watched the house for hours, but nothing was happening. Then we got a call from Grampa.

"The hen has flown the coop!" said Grampa.

Sure enough, Gramma was leaving the house, and she was carrying an armful of cookbooks.

42

We followed Gramma into town and realized, to our surprise, all of the old ladies of Gingham County were marching into the Star Curls beauty parlor.

"They're all carrying cookbooks," said Jubal. "Must be some sort of midnight bake-off."

CHAPTER 8

Aliens Are a Drag

"We've got to find a way to sneak into that beauty shop," said Grampa.

"You'll never get in there," said a mysterious voice from behind us.

It was Leslie the hairdresser.

"I've been watching them from across the street all night. You gotta be a grandma to get into that joint."

That gave me an idea. "Leslie, could you use your stellar beautician skills to turn us into grannies?"

"For shizzle!" said Leslie.

So Leslie helped disguise us as grandmas. Jubal got a big black bun and a polka-dot dress.

I got a pink frock and a string of pearls.

Javier, Leslie's assistant, gave Merle the granny treatment.

But Grampa was Leslie's masterpiece.

"All right," I said. "Remember, when we infiltrate the beauty shop, we have to act like hypnotized grannies. Don't show any emotion. Are there any questions?"

"I just have one question," said Grampa. "Does this dress make my butt look fat?"

CHAPTER 9

Fortress of the Grannies

We grabbed some cookbooks and marched into the spooky beauty salon. We fit right in with the other grannies. The place was huge and super high-tech. Madam Greed lorded over everything, in her floating La-Z-Boy.

Gramma and her friends were being squirted
with gooey hair products. Their hairdos seemed
to grow and pulsate before our very eyes.

PLEASE DON'T
FEED THE
HUMANS

In another room, we spotted a bunch of giant cages. A few of them even had people in them.

"Look, there's old man Jorgensen," said Grampa. "I was wondering why I didn't see him at rugby practice yesterday."

Madam Greed gathered the army of grannies together: "Elderly women of Earth. The weapons test last night proved to be a great success. We launch our full-scale attack tomorrow night at nine, right after *America's Top Supermodels*."

"Full-scale attack," said Grampa. "I don't like the sound of that. Thank goodness we blend in with these ladies. They don't suspect a thing."

CHAPTER 10

Uh-Oh!

Unfortunately, Merle decided it was time to give himself a cat bath.

"Wait a minute!" yelled Madam Greed. "Why is that human licking her own foot?"

"Oh, that's just Mertyle," said Grampa. "She's always lickin' those feet. She's got terrible foot fungus. I'd keep my distance if I were you."

"Seize those impostors!" yelled Greed. "There's only one way to make sure they're real grandmas. Give them the mayonnaise test!"

To my horror, one of the women brought out a
jar of mayonnaise.

"Now, everyone knows that all grandmas can eat
a spoonful of mayonnaise without flinching,"
said Greed.

Grampa got the first spoonful. "Um! Delicious,"
he said.

Jubal was next. "Thank you, ma'am. May I have
another?" he said bravely.

I was surprised that Merle
scarfed down his spoonful
of mayo. Of course, Merle
has been known to eat the
legs off of june bugs.

Then came the moment I was dreading—my
turn. In case you haven't heard, I'd rather eat
a fire-ant sandwich than eat mayonnaise.

The glassy-eyed granny approached me with
the quivering spoonful of that evil substance
and shoved it in my mouth. It sat on my tongue
for a second like a salty slug and then...

I spit it everywhere! I couldn't help it. The grannies were distracted by the shower of mayo, so I decided to make a run for it.

"Come on, boys!" I screamed. "Let's get out of here!"

CHAPTER 11

Extreme Earth Makeover

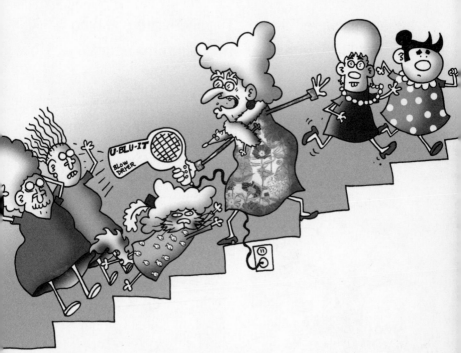

Grampa held off the grannies with a hair dryer while we ran for it.

"Back, you batty old biddies!" yelled Grampa. "Don't make me whip out my curling iron!"

We managed to escape the grannies by slipping into a storage room—or at least, we thought it was a storage room. We turned around to discover a giant globe of the earth and a bunch of blueprints.

"Holy mackerel!" I said. "The aliens are planning to turn Earth into an enormous intergalactic country diner!"

"Well, we could use another place to eat around here," said Grampa.

Just then, the grannies discovered where we were!

"Look!" I yelled. "An unidentified alien tentacle
is slipping under the door! Let's escape through
that window, quick!"

We escaped the evil beauty parlor, ditched our disguises, and hid in an alley. We had lost our alien pursuers.

"We've got to warn the rest of Gingham County about the alien attack," I said.

"But who's gonna believe us?" asked Jubal.

"We have evidence," I said, pulling out a bottle of alien hair-product. "I managed to swipe this before we left."

"Good work, Wiley," said Grampa. "Now, let's go home and get out of these heels. My feet are killing me."

CHAPTER 12

Alien Slime Is Fun

The next day, we took the bottle to Nate Farkles for analysis.

"Thanks for doing this on such short notice," I told Nate.

"No problem, boys," said Nate. "This beats looking at dog slobber all day."

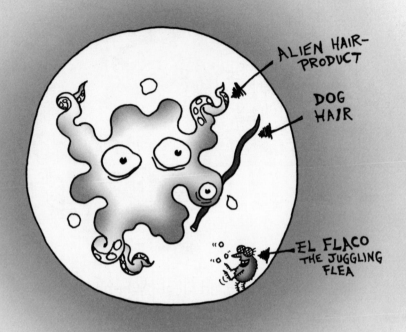

ALIEN HAIR-PRODUCT

DOG HAIR

EL FLACO
THE JUGGLING FLEA

Nate slid a sample of the slimy goop under the microscope.

"Wow!" said Nate. "This is some hair-product. It's actually a living, growing life-form. Look at the way it absorbs and takes over these samples of hair. Plus, it cures dandruff and smells like fresh honeysuckle! What will they come up with next?"

"Hey, look at this," said Jubal. "When I hold the bottle under this ultraviolet light, it changes from *Warm Sierra Rain Wash* to *Warm Sierra **Brain** Wash*!"

"Alien-brainwashed grannies," I said. "We've got to warn the town. We'll meet tonight at eight in the town hall. Spread the word!"

CHAPTER 13

Spreadin' the Word

So, that day, we let everyone know about our secret meeting. Jubal and I told the boys at soccer practice.

Morbius told his fellow nerd brethren.

Esther and Chavez informed the pooches down
at the doggy spa.

And Grampa let the boys down at the park
know—actually, Grampa napped.

CHAPTER 14

Stay Calm!

That night, everyone gathered at town hall.
Mayor Maynott tried his best to calm the crowd.

"Please, everyone remain calm!" said the mayor.
"Wiley and Grampa have important information
regarding the recent attacks by elderly women.
Let's give it up for Grampa! Woo! Woo! Woo!"

"Everybody just relax! There is no reason to panic," said Grampa. "By the way, an evil alien hairdresser has brainwashed the grandmas of Gingham County and they plan to attack and capture us tonight, right after *America's Top Supermodels*. Then they'll turn the earth into a giant country diner. We gathered this information last night when we went out at midnight dressed as old women."

"Yes, it's true!" said a voice from the back of the auditorium.

It was Madam Greed and her brainwashed grannies. "My real name is Madam Slorzog, and the citizens of my planet, Smorgasborg, are sick of fast-food joints. They want a new diner with down-home country cookin'. The grandmas of Gingham County are the best cooks in the business."

"Hey!" said Jubal. "It's only eight o'clock. Weren't you supposed to attack after *America's Top Supermodels?*"

"I'm TiVo-ing it as we speak," said Madam Slorzog.

"Wait a minute," I said. "How did you know we were meeting here?"

"Sorry, guys. It was me," said Nate Farkles. "Shortly after you left my lab, the grannies showed up and gave me their special brain-washing hair treatment."

"I thought your hair looked different," said Grampa. "So radiant and shiny. It's a good look."

"But what do you plan to do with the rest of us?" asked little Amy Pennington.

"We'll probably be forced to work as dishwashers and busboys in their astro slophouse!" I said angrily.

"Oh, it's better than that," said Madam Slorzog. "If you look closely at these cookbooks, we've crossed out all the meat and replaced it with humans!"

"You mean...you're gonna eat us?" asked Jubal.

"Yes," said Madame Slorzog. "It's all part of our new ad campaign on planet Smorgasborg.'"

"I'd like to take this opportunity to point out that I'm high in cholesterol and full of sharp bones that are easy to choke on," said Grampa.

CHAPTER 15

Crouching Nerd, Hidden Oddball

"Oh, no, you don't!" yelled Morbius, who burst in with his fellow nerds. "If you want to eat the good citizens of Gingham County, you're gonna have to deal with us first. I must warn you, we have mastered all thirty-six chambers of Shaolin!"

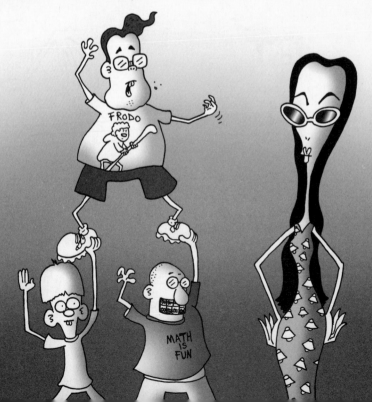

"Oh, you silly boys," said Madam Slorzog as the grannies brought out desserts, "why fight when you could enjoy some delicious pie and cupcakes instead?"

"Wow! Cupcakes!" exclaimed Morbius as he and his fellow nerds went for the pastries.

The pastries, of course, attacked the nerds with full force.

"Aaarghh!" screamed Morbius. "Defeated by my own sweet tooth! Carry on without us, brothers and sisters! Never give up the fight!"

"I thought nerds were supposed to be smart," said Grampa.

CHAPTER 16

When Grammas Attack

The attack had begun! Madam Slorzog marched her army of grannies through town, armed with

their arsenal of remote-control pies, flying teapots, killer yarn balls, and other homemade weapons. A large mechanical claw captured fleeing citizens and plopped them into a big cage.

"This is gonna be terrible for tourism!" yelled the mayor.

But we decided to fight back. Jubal did a powerful roundhouse kick and shattered the attacking toxic teapots.

Grampa made a delicious snack of the dive-bombing pies.

Merle ripped the killer knittings to shreds with his razor-sharp cat claws.

"It's gonna take more than attacking appliances and killer crafts to defeat us!" I yelled as I wrestled a voracious vacuum cleaner.

CHAPTER 17

Gee, Your Hair Looks Horrific!

"If you say so!" said Madam Slorzog. "Now I'll show you the awesome power of my Warm Sierra Brain Wash!"

Then she said something in her native Smorgasborgian: *"Clapto Sluggus Niptuk!"*

The grannies' hairdos started to pulsate and grow to a gargantuan size!

Then Gramma's hair sprouted giant slimy tentacles. Cleta Van Snout's hair sported a huge laser-shooting eyeball and Willie Mae Brown's hair shot out bolts of electricity! All the old ladies had killer monster do's!

The monster hair was too much for us to deal
with. The town was at the mercy of Gramma
and her big-haired buddies.

"Well, I guess this is it," said Grampa.
"Captured like wild animals, only to be served
up in a cosmic cafeteria. I only hope they turn
me into an attractive entrée with lots of gravy!"

"Wait a minute!" I said. "I've got an idea. It's time to fight hair with hair. Merle, I need one of your world-famous hair balls, quick!"

Most people don't know that Merle can sometimes hack up a hair ball on command. He can also juggle kitty-litter clumps and meow the alphabet.

Merle snorted and wheezed, then leaned over and hacked up an impressive hair ball with extra mucus.

I took the bottle of Warm Sierra Brain Wash and dumped all of it on the hair ball.

Then I chanted, "*Klapto Sluggis Nipto* or something like that!"

The hair ball began to grow and jiggle.

Then it grew to an enormous size and came to life!

Merle commanded his mutant hairy offspring to attack Madam Slorzog. The gloppy beast engulfed her in one swoop.

"Yikes!" she yelped. "You may have captured me, but you still have my alien-grandma army to deal with!"

"Just leave that to me, sister!" It was Leslie the hairdresser, and she was armed with mousse, hair gel, and super-hold hair spray. "Here ya go, people! Aim for their noggins! These ladies are about to have a bad hair day!"

We used the hair gel, mousse, and hair spray to immobilize the wild hair monsters. Gramma's hair tentacles froze up under the weight of the mega-hold hair spray.

Cleta tried to zap us with her hair laser, but Leslie's gem sweater was impervious to her dangerous beams. Leslie retaliated with a healthy dose of hair spray.

With their big hair immobilized, the grannies were powerless. That's when Grampa and Javier jumped in with the hair clippers.

"Let's get rid of those hair **don'ts**!" said Grampa as he sheared off the monstrous hair from Gramma and the gang.

Without their alien-infested hair, the grannies snapped back to normal, and boy, were they mad about their shaved heads.

"Sorry, ladies," cried Madam Slorzog. "I was just following orders. The leader of Smorgasborg wants restaurant construction completed by next month. In fact, he's arriving tomorrow morning to check my progress and he wants a taste test."

"If it's a taste test he wants," I declared, "then it's a taste test he'll get! Come on, everyone, we're heading to the Gingham County Elementary lunchroom! I know just the lunch lady who can help us."

"Vera, the lunch lady?" asked Jubal. "Haven't we had enough slime and suffering for one day?"

CHAPTER 18

Now We're Cookin'

We headed over to the school cafeteria, where Vera was already hard at work creating her next lunch atrocity.

"Vera, we need your help!" I yelled.

"Wait a minute!" said Jubal. "Her hair is awfully big. How do we know she isn't possessed by aliens?"

GINGHAM ELEMENTARY
KITCHEN

- GAS MASKS SHOULD BE WORN AT ALL TIMES.
- SLOPPY JOES MUST BE SERVED AT LEAST TWICE A WEEK!
- EMPLOYEES MUST NOT WASH HANDS BEFORE RETURNING TO WORK
- EXPIRATION DATES ARE FOR WIMPS

"It's okay, sweetie. This is a wig," said Vera. "I lost my real hair in the Great Hot Wax Explosion of 1943."

"Vera," I said. "No time for chitchat. You've gotta start cooking. We need five of your most disgust—I mean—delicious entrées by eight o'clock tomorrow morning. The fate of the planet is in your Crock-Pot!"

In the morning, we all gathered in the backyard to await our interstellar guest.

"I still don't get it, Wiley," said Grampa. "How is Vera's cooking going to save our planet?"

"It's simple," I said. "Vera's cuisine is so disgusting that after just one taste, their alien leader will spontaneously throw up and then get as far away from Earth as possible!"

CHAPTER 19

Gross Encounters of the Lard Kind

At eight o'clock sharp, a giant spaceship burst through the clouds and landed in front of us.

A very large alien stepped out of the ship.

"Ladies and Gentlemen," said Madam Slorzog,
"I present to you the president of planet Smorgasborg,
award-winning author, and three-time Universal
Ping-Pong champion, Mr. Slobba the Hut."

"Greetings," said Slobba. "Where's the grub?"

"The last thing that boy needs is a new restaurant,"
whispered Grampa.

Slobba sat down for his meal and Vera quickly served up some grade-A gruel. Slobba sniffed the slop and then took a big bite. He swished it around in his mouth and then froze.

He then began to go into convulsions! Fire shot out of his ears!

"It's okay, mister," I said. "I've prepared a giant-size barf bag for you. I know how disgusting this meal must be for you."

"Disgusting?" Slobba yelled. "Why, this is the most scrumptious food I've ever tasted! It's incredible! It's stupendous! It's pretty darn good! Humans are delicioso!"

It looked like my plan had backfired.

Luckily, Vera stepped in. "Actually, there are no humans in my cooking. I use only the freshest ingredients from the local trash heap."

"Forget about the restaurant," said Slobba. "I want you to come to Smorgasborg to be my personal royal chef!"

"Well," said Vera. "I guess I could use a vacation."

"Hot dog!" said Slobba as a welcoming committee of aliens came and grabbed Vera. "Let's bounce!"

So, our alien guests took off with Vera and headed back into space.

"I'm gonna miss those Smorgasborgians," said Grampa. "I guess we'll never know what I'd taste like as a chicken-fried steak!"

CHAPTER 20

Hair Repair

So that's all there is. The kids in the school lunchroom took it pretty hard when they learned that Vera was gone. Actually, we threw a huge party.

But the party was cut short when we found out Vera had been replaced by her twin sister, Grizzelda.

TODAY'S SPECIAL
DUCK FEET WITH
MALT VINEGAR
+
CREAMED OKRA
DESSERT:
BAT GUANO
CRUMB CAKE

Leslie gave Gramma and the other old ladies some fancy new do's.

And, soon, Gramma was back to her cranky self, but I must admit, we never looked at her casseroles the same way again.

As for Merle's giant hair ball—it joined the Dangling Brothers Traveling Circus and became their star attraction.

Merle was so proud.

Famous director George Mucus has just filmed the exciting movie version of our alien adventure, but something went wrong when we printed up the posters. That second one looks funky. Help us pick out the differences before we hang 'em at the local cineplex.

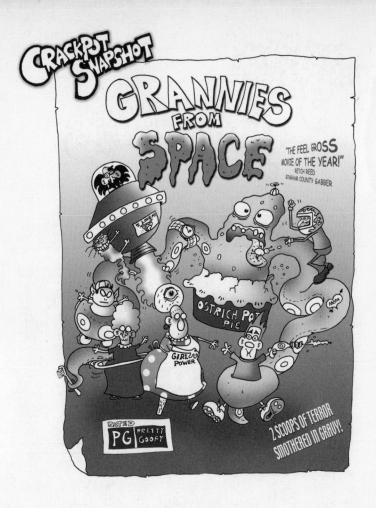

The answers are on the next page. Anyone caught cheating will be doused with evil alien hair products!